Photo
Finish

PHOTO
FINISH

Barbara Shrubsole

Matador
9 Priory Business Park,
Wistow Road, Kibworth Beauchamp,
Leicestershire. LE8 0RX
Tel: 0116 279 2299
Email: books@troubador.co.uk
Web: www.troubador.co.uk/matador
Twitter: @matadorbooks

ISBN 978 1789018 103

British Library Cataloguing in Publication Data.
A catalogue record for this book is available from the British Library.

Printed and bound by CPI Group (UK) Ltd, Croydon, CR0 4YY
Typeset in 11pt Aldine401 BT by Troubador Publishing Ltd, Leicester, UK

Matador is an imprint of Troubador Publishing Ltd

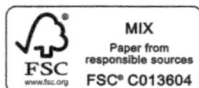

Simply to say
"Thank you."

Preface

Probably for you, as for the majority of people alive at the time, 1994 passed without anything happening that caused it to be held in memory as significantly marking a turning point in your life. However, there will be some for whom this is far from the case. It is true to a lesser or greater extent for the four people who, with others associated with them, will feature in this story:

Jason, Michael, David and Nancy

In 1994, they were not connected in any way; just two boys who, independently, celebrated their ninth birthdays during the year, a young man who could be described as "in his prime" and a much older lady, as the name is likely to suggest. How have their lives somehow become entangled years later?

Part One

Nancy

Nancy Ingram was brought up with what might be described as church values. Looking back, one could be excused for seeing this as a "Thou shalt not" way of life, having parents who tried to pass on to their only child the basics of a way of life that would ensure she fitted "nicely" into society.

Enter Harry.

How Harry had arrived on the scene remains somewhat clouded... suffice to say he had entered the home of the Ingram family. This had brought two new experiences into the life of this young man: the first, employment in this local family grocery store and the second, being expected to attend Sunday church services, neither of which suggested much excitement until, that is, he encountered Nancy in both areas, which resulted in an increased threefold level of commitment. Church picnics, social evenings, minimal attendance at the tennis club, organised walks... in fact, any event within church circles where liaising with the opposite sex was permitted. And surprise, surprise; the attraction seemed to be a two-way thing. How was it that Nancy always seemed to find herself walking near him or listening to his entertaining conversation and even, on occasion, noticing his eye contact during services? How did Harry, who definitely saw her as the most eligible female around, manage to volunteer to make an extra grocery delivery just at the moment when she would be returning home? Or how did he just happen to be around in the shop when Nancy needed something off a high shelf or something heavy carried? Could there even have been any ulterior motive of future involvement in the family firm? For Nancy, it was simply that a new excitement had arrived in what had been, up until then, a rather dull life. It was surprising that they managed to keep this increasing mutual attraction hidden from the close proximity of eyes that would have undoubtedly disapproved. Why, you may ask, when Harry always presented himself as hard-working and well groomed, with excellent manners in contact both in the shop and the church fellowship? I suppose it could simply be described as the class differentials of society at that time… shop owner's daughter and goods delivery status. Nancy just saw what was in front of her and she liked it a lot.

There was, however, one area of Harry's life that she was almost desperate to keep away from her parents' knowledge… the fact that Harry was known, on occasion, to frequent the newly opened betting shop in the High Street. The first time this had come to Nancy's notice was when they had unexpectedly encountered each other as he left said premises. She had pretended not to notice, but on another occasion, while walking together, he had politely excused himself and she had apparently engrossed herself in the nearby latest summer hat display while all the time managing to see where he went. It didn't really bother Nancy, although she harboured a curiosity as to what went on in these forbidden so-called "dens of iniquity"! That was indeed how she had heard the idea of betting shops described and indeed, gambling in any form was "no, no, no" in the rules of life, just about rating as a deadly sin. Recognising the situation and people involved, inevitably, something was going to have to give, and sure enough the moment arrived when Nancy was forced to make a choice:

The Somerset Stakes

Harry had tickets and invited Nancy to come and spend a day at the races with him. At first, it sounded impossible but… Saturday was a busy day for her father and mother in the shop and she was often free to spend the day with friends. If she planned it well, a bus to Bathampton, a picnic by the river and a gentle stroll back, or even a bit more time spent in a friend's home… while all the time, she could be with Harry in something exciting that he called "a day at the races", whatever that meant… and her parents need never know.

It was not in Nancy's nature to be devious, or perhaps the necessary skill required had never previously been put to the test, but with such possibilities at stake, she discovered her high level of intelligence proved more than adequate to ensure that she found herself walking on the arm of Harry towards the gathering company, while her parents remained in complete ignorance of their daughter's actual whereabouts. It is possible to find many photographs held in archives, recording the sights that confronted Nancy on that day. It is not difficult to imagine her excitement, tinged with perhaps a little apprehension, which caused her to grip Harry's arm a little more tightly. She was now actually part of something that she had previously only glimpsed as featured in newspapers.

She walked in a sort of dream state towards the race course itself, every step revealing more and more of this vibrant scene when people and horses come together at the races.

Time moved on through a succession of small preliminary races. Nancy, glued to Harry, observed as he placed a small amount of money on the table of a brightly clad person, watched the ensuing competitions that brought differing responses in Harry, heard the thunder of the horses' hooves and the cries of the crowd, all combining in rapidly escalating excitement as the start of the main race drew nearer. As promised, right hand now free to remove the secreted coins from her clutch bag, Harry now stood beside her as, apparently full of confidence, she placed her very first ever bet...

Future Promise... the name of the horse had caught her imagination and although not fully appreciated at the time, foretold of what was to become a part of her life.

Together they stood with those gathered on the raised grassy slope to ensure a good view. Unaware or bothered by anyone around, a totally uninhibited Nancy jumped up and down and shouted encouragement to Future Promise from the off until the moment when her horse passed the winning post in third place. Harry propelled an elated Nancy back to collect her small winnings and for an opportunity to stand together for a photograph near the horse. She remained in a joyful daze until at last, as they walked away, he managed to bring matters back to reality. As Nancy struggled to compose herself in order to calmly face her parents, she recognised that it had been a fantastic never-to-be-forgotten day with Harry. However, at this moment, she was unaware that a way to bring an unbelievable excitement into her mundane life had been ignited. Back home, Nancy was able to provide an acceptable muted account of her day and, pleading tiredness, withdrew to her bedroom early in preparation for the next day.

Most of us will have been what could be described as "economical with the truth" during our lives, with often disastrous results. Nancy had taken an incredible risk. She appeared to have got away with it, but sadly, as in most cases, the truth will out, which she discovered only too soon, when, two days later, she was summoned and duly found herself standing before "the court of one" – which could be the only way to describe it – as she stood before her father in the study.

'I forbid you to see that young man again!'

That was all that was said but, perhaps unbelievably now, at that time it was enough for his daughter to realise there was no point in trying to argue… Father's word was law and had to be obeyed. It was made somewhat easier by Harry's instant dismissal, accompanied by his rapidly leaving the area. The one bright spot in what seemed otherwise total blackness was when an unknown passer-by handed her a white envelope, and on opening it, she found it contained a photograph of her alongside Harry and a horse, clearly Future Promise. On the back was written a message: *Never to be forgotten. Love, Harry*. This was instantly secreted, with a few tears, in the back of a drawer, kept forever, for her observation only. One thing that did cause Nancy to wonder later was who, numbered amongst her father's so-called friends, had also visited the races on that fatal Saturday; but discovery would, by then, have been of no significance.

What has all this to do with 1994, since it happened so many years earlier?

Unlikely as it may seem, that one day, or to be more explicit, that one race, sparked off something that would present something new for Nancy, something that remained with her for the rest of her life and would provide the catalyst for the future of this story... the excitement surrounding placing a bet and then awaiting the result of the race. A spark that could come loosely under the heading, *Gambling*, had been ignited.

In no way could what followed be described as an addiction that would have had the ability to wreck her's and other's lives, but rather, she had the desire and found opportunities to experience that same excitement in a variety of ways. She had access to limited money from her allotted wages as she used book keeping skills for the firm and she had her own bank account. Using her intelligence and as a loving daughter, shall we say, avoiding causing her parents any anxiety, she found ways to brighten life. At first, it was purchasing previously forbidden raffle tickets and just occasionally winning a prize. It wasn't long before, using guidance from the newspaper in the library, she found a way, with assistance, to both place an occasional bet in the aforementioned premises and secretly receive any winnings. Perhaps the easiest and most regular excitement came when she became part of a football pools group... money paid in each week to an organiser, check for score draws each Saturday – always anticipating a big win – and infrequently receive a small cash return.

★

The years for Nancy passed in a fairly predictable way... the dutiful daughter in the small middle-class family. Social life? Limited but not really questioned, just accepted. Weekly meetings at the church with the occasional coach outing, bussing into town for purchasing special items and the once-a-year week-long family holiday to the same small hotel by the sea in Devon. Nancy had always enjoyed reading, and she continued to perhaps live another life through her books. At first, she continued to play her part in the shop, but her father's early death necessitated selling the business with its adjacent premises and moving to a semi-detached house in the village. Then followed devoted support for her mother, and although the more dominant presence of her father had been removed, Nancy's lifestyle had become, well, part of Nancy. She remained very much the same as observed by those around her. She was clearly very careful about how she looked, could be relied upon to use some of her extra time when volunteers were needed at the church and always had a friendly greeting for people in the village. General opinion... Nancy Ingram... she's a really nice lady. She did, however, take on a small part-time job in the local newsagent's.

It appeared this is how things would remain indefinitely until the events of 1994 brought significant change. Sadly, her mother's death in January meant that although Nancy was now a "free agent" with no restrictions, the removal of a regular day-to-day routine proved far from easy, bringing with it the challenge of life readjustment. Fortunately, Nancy was able, with the help of their long-time family bank manager, to sort out finances and, as an only daughter, practical matters fell into place. But as the year started on a low note, it ended on a high for Nancy when November 1994 marked the birth of the National Lottery.

Jason and Michael

The only significant way to link them together at the start of 1994 was that both boys were aged eight with birthdays just months apart… that is perhaps the sole sum of their likeness! To look at… one in desperate need of being "tidied up", topped off by tousled fair hair that would respond positively to both brush and scissors, while the other… well, quite the opposite, with everything in place!

Jason lived in Bath, but not in any way enjoying the benefits of being a resident in this heritage city as might be supposed, but rather in a household on a council estate on the fringes of the city… a household where shouting and arguing were the norm.

Michael's childhood was rooted further west, the son of middle-class parents who, while undoubtedly wanting the best for their only son, tended to wrap him in cotton wool.

Jason was never quite sure about his real dad. The story was that he had left when Jason was two, and from then on, there had been a succession of men whom he was encouraged to call Dad, each for a short time. His mum needed company and apparently had no trouble in attracting it with all that that entailed. A baby had arrived as an addition to the family with that "Dad" rapidly disappearing, leaving his mother even more harassed and Jason expected to act in a caring role from time to time when his mother went out as an escape. He had to cope, always feeling unwanted and so often in trouble as his mother lacked any guiding rules of life to share. She had not enough time, there was not enough room so he could never have space, and there was not enough money to go round. Life was not easy at home for Jason but what about outside?

School was a mixed blessing. He was popular and had plenty of friends as he would readily join in anything, finding the joy of belonging, even when it frequently got him into trouble. He was well known amongst the staff for all the wrong reasons, one of which being his increasing times of absence which, when followed up, always seemed to result in his mother's surprising apology and agreement to do better... until the next time!

The desire to read and write well held little attraction, although he found an occasional interest in what they called maths. But on the football field was a different matter; all his being was fully involved as, no doubt, in every moment he lived out the dreams of one day being a star. Being eight was certainly not easy for Jason.

In a strange way, the same could be said of Michael.

Michael's father had huge future plans for his son and probably his mother quietly acquiesced. It was in no doubt that they were devoted parents seeking, in their eyes, the very best for their son. They could manage to pay for his education, ensuring that he met the right people. Michael was regularly taken to places that might educate him further.

Unfortunately, boy and plan did not match. Perhaps it could be identified as a case of father attempting to live out his dreams through his son. Michael, even at this early age, did not appear to resemble his father's side of the family. He was slight in build and in nature rather shy, hardly surprising with an overpowering father. He hated the premise at the school, even at this early age, that everyone should love rugby. He was helped out in this area when it was discovered he was short-sighted and needed glasses. His friends were limited to a few who loved studying, but unfortunately, Michael's level of achievement in this area also fell short of his father's expectation. Suffice to say, he was guarded against the knocks of life that Jason experienced. The future seemed to have been well planned with little reference to him. Extra study was always at the forefront, with the constant reminder that the time was getting near when he would have to gain a place in the senior section of the school. He had never been encouraged, or even given a chance, to challenge decisions by thinking for himself, and the signs were already in evidence pointing to future problems.

While life apparently continued much the same for Michael, for Jason, 1994 provided a major turning point when Steve moved in, claiming his mother's affections... another so-called "Dad", but on this occasion it was worse because he brought with him a ready-made "younger brother" for Jason. Had the boys been closer in age it might have worked, but Steve's son, Darren, no doubt having already experienced a far from settled life, certainly knew how to make things difficult for his new "elder brother"!

DAVID

While Steve's arrival in 1994 marked the year for Jason, across the other side of the city of Bath, something quite dramatic was about to happen for the fourth member of our quartet.

David Spriggs and Michelle were recognised as a partnership. They had been living together for some time, with life following a more or less settled path, but all that was about to change.

David returned from work in the normal way to find a clearly purposeful Michelle waiting for him.

'Sit down, David.'

For once, he really looked at her… the firmness in the three words demanded attention.

'I'm pregnant.'

And he sat down.

Other people heard these words but not him. Since they'd been living together, they'd been careful… well, he'd left it to Michelle… and now she was pregnant.

He was going to be a father!

Suddenly the thought motor in his brain took off, racing from one thing to another, failing to find any comprehensive words. His power of speech was frozen. Time was frozen.

Michelle didn't move. She stood waiting for his response, her face expressionless, giving no indication of her inner uncertainty of how this news would be received. What would happen next?

David's eyes rested on the area of her body that concealed his son… his son.

He was going to be a dad!

The reality of the situation was taking hold and the ice was melting, slowly at first, then more quickly, then rapidly… so rapidly that he sprang up from the chair and wrapped his strong arms around Michelle and hugged her to him. They clung together in a moment that needed no words.

★

'Will you take this man to be your lawful wedded husband?'

Her childhood dreams of a fairy-tale wedding had been shattered. She realised only too well now that's what it had been… just fairy-tale dreams… real life didn't work like that.

As she stood in the pleasant but somewhat restricted space of the registry office, Michelle said farewell to the dreams of a fairy-tale wedding forever. She smiled at the man standing beside her and could only give thanks that he hadn't walked away on hearing of her unexpected pregnancy. The suggestion that they should get married had come from him. The suit and tie made him appear quite handsome. What right had she to talk about good looks? She so hoped she looked okay.

She had chosen the loose dress to hopefully conceal her increasing waistline. The hat felt like the one link to what might have been… a waste of money perhaps, but it was something special for her.

David had been used to people making jokes about his employment. With friends, it was okay, but it was never easy to respond to new acquaintances.

'I drive a refuse vehicle', which in itself sounded a little better than a "dustbin lorry"!

The truth remained that working for the council had proved a life-saver for him and Michelle.

Their daughter, Louise, arrived into the security of a family home. At that time it was a flat in a not-too-exciting part of the city, a tenancy that went with the job.

David had tried several things when he had left school, all fairly short term but each providing the necessary money while he was still living at home… home where, he said, he had been fortunate to learn so much of what is important in life; a simple background where he knew he was loved. He had found the job at the refuse depot quite by chance while helping an elderly neighbour. Much to his and his parents' surprise, he liked it. At first, it had been physical work around the recycling containers within the depot. Management had fortunately recognised value in him as an employee and had arranged for him to go out with the lorries while, at the same time, allowing for driving instruction and qualification.

All this had taken time and David would be the first to say that Michelle had provided what he needed to ensure that he did not give up when something annoying occurred. You have already heard about the greatest challenge that had come into David's life so far and the way he responded, and how more lives are added to the story.

David and Michelle worked as a team, building their life together, fully recognising the responsibility of parenthood. Conscious of the ever-present need for money to pay bills, Michelle found a way to help. David's regular hours allowed for her to work evenings in the local supermarket with, thankfully, the occasional babysitting help from grandparents when David had the opportunity of overtime.

Louise had three causes for celebration in 1998: a third birthday, a baby brother and a new home with a garden.

Johnathan David, the son David had secretly hoped for, brought both joy and more challenges to this young family but once again they coped. They now qualified for a three-bedroom council house and were delighted when they were offered a property not too far from where they lived at present. David's journey to work was about the same, Michelle would hopefully be able to return to her checkout job sometime, and Louise had her own pink bedroom and a secure garden to play in. JD, as he became known, just seemed to fit in and started smiling very early in his life.

So now you have the picture of life for the Spriggs family as they move on through the next few years, experiencing very much the normal expected ups and downs in providing for growing children in a happy environment... nursery days then school; a house comfortably untidy at times but always welcoming to friends; birthday and Christmas celebrations and the looked-forward-to annual caravan holiday by the sea… all in all, certainly more laughter than tears.

Michael

The path for Michael was clearly mapped out in his father's mind. Perhaps it would be correct to say his parents' minds, as his mother seemed to have accepted her role in agreeing with her dominant partner to ensure peace within the household. She recognised that her husband's intention was good; trying to ensure their son had all the benefits in life that had been unavailable to them. Philip, who had achieved so much against the odds with no private education or university, but simply as a result of his determination and hard work, clearly thought he could now use his success to make things easier for his son. Unfortunately, life so often doesn't fit into an apparently logical plan.

The path for Michael was indeed clearly marked out. At first, it involved all that was needed to ensure a place in the senior section of the school. To say Michael suffered would be an exaggeration, but there was definitely little time left for anything Michael might choose, which sadly included forming any real friendship with a classmate. Any time spent with boys of his own age out of school hours revolved around families of his father's acquaintances who could be described as "the right sort of people". There was always the pressure to achieve academically, only too obvious when it was noted as a moment of great family celebration – well, really for one member – Michael gaining his place in the senior section. Perhaps if his mother had been more confident, things might have been different. Who knows? There is no such thing as hindsight, just a gradual life learning curve until … as in this case, something gives way.

Having made it into the main school, Michael just managed, with a struggle, to keep in the top set for maths – which pleased his father – was passable at English, naturally preferring the reading to the writing, but showed little or no interest in science or sport. While not displaying any musical talent himself, Michael enjoyed listening to classical music, and this was the one after school club he joined. Physically, he grew taller and remained slight of build. Contrary to many of his contemporaries, he was always clean and tidy with perfect manners, as would be expected in his situation. Again, in contrast to most boys his age, he became more and more quiet and withdrawn; something that did not go completely unnoticed by his mother. School reports and open evenings emphasised what a nice young man he was, a pleasure to have in the classroom with generally only "fair" comments about his academic achievement that should have opened eyes and ears regarding the future. Sadly, his father's dream clouded any clear thinking.

The word "examinations", with all that meant for individual members of this family, loomed ever nearer… all-round pressure and stress… and something had to give, and give it did!

A turning point had arrived in Michael's life.

A phone call brought Mother and then also Father to the school, summoned by information that Michael had collapsed.

This was not a medical collapse needing a 999 call but rather a mental cry for help, having succumbed at length to the horror of failure in life ahead. He had given his best, struggling through in the GCSE preparation but now, aged sixteen, the incessant talk of A-levels and university was just too much. Fortunately, on this particular morning, his housemaster came forward in his support but, more to the point, his mother spoke out with surprising confidence. For once, his father was stunned into silence. He agreed, with direction from his wife, that they needed time together as a family... time in which to discover the best way ahead for Michael.

Conversations, discussions, differing opinions, arguments and tears filled the household during the next few days. Eventually, decisions were made and agreed. Further education establishments, of any sort, would definitely play no further part.

They would await results of the exams with the possibility of discovering an apprenticeship opportunity or finding a suitable job situation. No need at this point to provide any documented information relating to detail. One thing, hardly surprising, is that Michael's father had a hand in the outcome; however, the real surprise came in that a now less pressurised Michael was pretty happy about life and agreed to the suggested way ahead.

★

This decision would actually bring Michael to the city where Nancy, Jason and David lived.

True to form, Michael's father grabbed the opportunity to contact a friend from schooldays who was now a bank manager in the city of Bath, and two weeks later, he found himself travelling, with a somewhat ulterior motive and not a little trepidation, to meet up again with Frank.

'Well, this is a surprise!'... handshake... 'Come in and sit down, Philip. I'll get Sandra to bring us some coffee, or would you prefer something stronger?'

'Thank you. Coffee would be fine.'

Philip sat down tentatively on the chair indicated, his usual show of confidence completely absent. He found himself facing Frank, whose demeanour clearly showed quite the opposite.

They had known each other as young men in a youth club friendship where they experienced a lot in common, disregarding any difference in background, centring more on hopes and dreams.

School years over, with each going their own way, they had kept in touch. At first, this meant the occasional meeting, but gradually, after being guests at weddings, drifting apart into the annual Christmas card and "we must meet up sometime" contact.

Philip, however, recognised that here might just be the help he needed... an opportunity to renew their friendship while, at the same time, obtaining a way ahead for Michael.

Never short of a plan, he had contacted Frank, requesting a meeting, which resulted in his finding himself in these affluent surroundings.

Frank obviously went out of his way to clearly show all visitors his status as a bank manager.

As if on cue, coffee and biscuits arrived and then...

'So what's this all about? Something to do with your son?' (Name clearly eluding him!)

'Thank you so much for seeing me like this. Yes, it's about Michael, like I said in the letter.'

'Right. Remind me. How old is he now?'

Philip, aware that the letter was not to hand, remained calm as he endeavoured to enlighten Frank with its contents and ...

'So what you're really saying is that you wonder if there is any chance that he could come and work here?'

Philip noticeably winced.

'Put bluntly, yes,' adding quickly, 'I have discussed this with Michael and he is happy for my meeting you.'

'How did his GCSEs go? Any A-C's?'

'Five in all, including B in maths.'

'And he really thinks he would like working in a bank?'

'They had one of those job fairs at the school, and he spoke well of banking afterwards.' Then, after a pause, he added, 'His mother and I had hoped he might go to university but the school advised otherwise.'

There ensued one of those awkward pauses with both men searching for the way ahead while relying on the aid of a cup of coffee and a shortbread biscuit.

'Well,' the space having been filled with memories, 'if Michael's happy, I think we could give it a try.'

Philip's tense lip line melted as, rising from his seat, he moved forward and grasped the proffered hand with considerable force.

'Thank you so much, Frank. I can't tell you how much this means to me. I'm sure Michael won't let you down.'

Both were smiling now.

'We'll work at it together... there's plenty of help available at the local college or through correspondence courses once we've settled in together.'

Philip made a move towards the door but Frank hadn't finished.

'If you haven't got to rush off, just give me five minutes and we could go and have a spot of lunch together. Few years to catch up on.'

Philip nodded his agreement.

Michael was about to move to Bath.

Jason

Jason never referred to Steve as Dad. The relationship was no go from the start, and there was never going to be any brotherly love with Steve's son, Darren, who was part of the package. Numbers facilitated a change of accommodation and a new school. This could have meant an opportunity for a new start for Jason, but just as he found himself at the bottom of the pile at home, so failure loomed at school as problems escalated.

Like to like, he quickly attached himself to a small group who had no interest in achieving academically. He rapidly became the "big fish" in the group and his behaviour deteriorated. There might have been a glimmer of hope when he moved into senior school, but sadly things did not go well and the negative spiral continued. By then his acquired desire for power was aided by a marked increase in physique, and it was not long before his actual attendance really deteriorated.

In desperation to turn things round, school punishment resulted in exclusion from any football involvement, the one area that just might have blossomed, which, of course, just made things worse. Attempts to establish a rapport between school and home also met with failure.

At home, it was obvious that he came last in his mother's affections as she wanted to impress this new partner, and Jason got in the way. He had to share a bedroom with his younger brother.

Jason had no space to call his own, was constantly being blamed for anything that went wrong, was shouted at and was even the recipient of Steve's aggression, more and more apparent on the latter's return from the pub. Steve, unfortunately, unlike some of the others, seemed a fixture, with Jason being left sort of in charge when his mother joined in the occasional pub visit.

The one thing that brought brightness into Jason's life over these years was when he spent Saturdays with his mother's Aunt Vera and they enjoyed time together, especially when that meant going to jumble sales... hardly what you would expect as a highlight in the life of a young man.

And then to crown it all, Aunt Vera died.

Jason could perhaps be best described as a simmering pot, gradually moving towards boiling point when the contents would overflow. Overflow they did... when, in the playground, Jason reacted violently towards a fellow pupil, inflicting damage on both the boy and one of the three members of staff needed to restrain him.

What happened next? The continuation of the spiralling, ever more rapidly, downwards.

Exclusion from school, his mother's admission of her inability to cope, social services' involvement, home visits and support, an extra education facility with personal encouragement, recognition of possible danger and risk in the family home, being taken into the care of the authority, trials with several different foster parents, all resulting, despite considerable effort and opportunity, in a young man totally at odds with society!

What else?

Mini brushes with the law, a spell in a young offenders' institution followed by a period of community service.

Sadly, the "fingers and toes crossed" of several involved did not bring about the desired result, and after sleeping on a variety of acquaintances' floors or rough around the city, Jason at length became a resident in the local homeless shelter.

Perhaps one of the most surprising things was that Jason never became a statistic in the drug scene.

★

In the middle of the year 2005, light dawned unexpectedly into previous despair. Light came in the form of a young nurse who became part of the health support team for night shelter residents. From the first meeting, he had been attracted and, while he did not have a need for official consultation, had taken to sort of being there when she paused for a welcome cup of tea. He had taken trouble to tidy himself a bit and had at first just smiled. The smile had been acknowledged and they had shared limited conversation together.

He had discovered her name was Joanne and he had taken to thinking about her while attempting to sleep; thoughts which invariably ended in a desire to find his way back into society.

Nancy

The birth of the Lottery provided an easy way to supply the, up'til then, secretly managed "buzz" in Nancy's life. She just purchased a ticket each week, very easily done with the continuation of involvement in the newsagent's, and watched the television on Saturday evening, always with the expectation of 'This could be my day!'

Another obvious change, hardly noted by visitors, was the appearance of a framed photograph of two people with a horse that now had pride of place on the sideboard alongside her parents' wedding photo. Indeed, anyone prompted to enquire about this would just receive a gentle smile and an 'Oh, just a memory from the past' response. Nobody knew that before placing this treasured item in its frame, Nancy had added her carefully chosen significant lottery numbers to the written message on the back.

Once the year was over, and now on her own, Nancy really enjoyed life.

She took full advantage of the invitation to join the "University of the Third Age", or U3A as it is better known. She joined the weekly simple fitness class in the sports centre and the gardening group, with regular talks and visits to gardens and just a very low level of practical gardening herself. Somehow this led on to a link being established between this group and flower arranging, a new skill that she shared in the church where, of course, there was always the weekly prayer gathering as well as the early morning Sunday service.

Flowers also gave her the opportunity for something very new: a first passport and a coach holiday to Holland to see the tulips. This was another opening for Nancy, awakening a previously unknown interest in travelling.

The two mornings at the shop meant that she was well known in the village. It was true to say that people agreed with the early hopes of her parents. Nancy was indeed a very nice lady.

And then something – the unexpected-but-secretly-hoped-for – happened for Nancy… One Saturday, her numbers and those randomly chosen as shown on the TV screen, matched!

Nancy avoided any publicity and relied once again on help at that moment, and for any future guidance regarding investment from her trusted bank manager. Nancy became an overnight multi-millionaire, and she would have more than enough money to spare for the rest of her life. But even the steady Mr Johnson was in for a surprise request initiated by this lady sometime later.

MICHAEL

On a few evenings, Michael had started going to the King William for a meal after work. It was conveniently nearby. Evenings in the hostel were long and, although he was not really a social being, it felt better to eat amongst others. He'd tried quite a few places in town but this pub did a pretty cheap meal. He could stay as long as he liked and read the evening paper.

When a group of guys, who seemed to be regulars, spoke to him, it seemed best to join in conversation with them, although he hoped he would be able to escape by inventing a prearranged engagement. He'd actually seen one of them last week in the bank.

'Okay if we sit here, mate?'

Quite an unnecessary question as the three young men, definitely not quite his type, now occupied the previously empty chairs. Michael, having chosen to sit right in the corner, nodded and then attempted to continue to devote his attention towards the pasty and the newspaper, all the time hoping that he wouldn't be expected to join in any conversation.

No such luck!

Rapidly, he was required to shake in turn the three proffered hands belonging to Dan, Rob and Rick.

'You new here?'

'Fairly.'

'Haven't seen you in here before. This your local?'

'Sort of.'

'You live near here then?'

'Sort of.'

Up to now they seemed to have shared in the questions, but Michael already had the feeling that one member of the group was dominant, and this seemed to be confirmed with the tone of the next response.

'What sort of answer is that?' and continuing while displaying a facial expression that said a lot, 'Sort of! Sort of!' and, obviously expecting more, 'What does "sort of" mean?'

'I live here during the week and usually go back home at weekends.' Michael answered quickly in the hope that this would satisfy and that he might be left alone.

He continued to address his food as if his very life depended on it, acknowledging that that was just what it actually felt like, making sure he avoided eye contact with any of his companions.

Respite for a few moments as two gave time to each other, while the third went to the bar for more drinks.

Then together again: 'You work here?'

'Yes.' Sadly, not enough.

'Where's that then?'

Michael experienced a very brief "do I tell them the truth?" moment before hearing himself reply, 'The bank.'

'Lucky you! Any chance of some free samples?'

More laughter and a "need to get to know you better" throw away comment. Then a follow-up question: 'Down in town?'

'No, the bank in the village.' Might as well stick with honesty.

'Have to pay you a visit!' …sounded just like a threat to Michael's ears.

'Well, where's it going to be then?' Miraculously, conversation amongst the trio.

'That new place up the top of town?'

Michael listened as they rattled off a variety of venues, each accompanied by a plus or minus.

Finally, they came to an agreement and then turning to Michael, 'D'you want to come with us, mate?' Pause and then, 'Bloody hell! I don't even know your name!'

Quick response: 'It's Michael and no, thank you. I've got something arranged.'

His companions fortunately seemed to accept this.

They stood up with a scraping of chairs and each proceeded to exchange a most ostentatious shake of hands with him before finally moving off, thankfully leaving with just an instruction to 'Look after those pounds!'

The 'See you again, mate,' as they exited the door received a non-verbal, *Not if I can help it,* from Michael.

Nancy

If ever anywhere could be described as a typical bank manager's office, this was it. The brown leather upholstery and large rectangular oak desk, so out of place in the present-day minimalist furnishing, immediately transported one out of the mundane into a place shouting of importance. Perhaps an instant picture would be best conveyed by simply saying *Dad's Army*. The small staff could be forgiven for adding that their well-loved but voice-from-the-past manager would not be out of place in that production.

It was a small facility serving the south of the city, and for many years, residents in the area had enjoyed the personal touch provided by Mr Johnson and the availability of banking facilities that did not necessitate a journey into the city centre.

'Come in and sit down, Nancy. My, you're looking well.'

'Thank you, Mr Johnson, for finding time for me in your busy schedule.'

'Always time for a treasured customer… after all, your family have banked with us for a very long time.'

'Indeed. Your predecessor was so kind to Mother when Father died. Made such a difference.

And then, when she passed on, you were here for me.'

'Lovely lady. Lovely lady. Tower of strength in this community for sure… a role which, if you don't mind my saying, you now fill yourself.'

Nancy responded with her characteristic smile.

Any possible response was interrupted by a knock at the door.

'That'll be Michael. I asked him to bring us in a pot of tea… makes business so much more pleasurable. Come in.'

Nancy watched the young man carry in the "pleasurable requirements". He placed the shiny tray almost reverently in the central space on the manager's desk.

'I expect you'll see Michael outside in the main office. He's one of our newest cashiers hoping to make a career in banking.'

Nancy smiled inwardly. Nothing about this young man suggested that he was cut out for the present day cut-throat world of banking. She had come here about money and she did not need a cup of tea as an aid to her business. She just had to remain firm when Mr Johnson tried, as he undoubtedly would, to get her to think again.

Rose-decorated china cup duly filled, sugar and biscuit declined.

'Now, Nancy, what was it you wanted to discuss?'

'I want to withdraw some money,' and after a short pause, she added, 'a lot of money.'

Eventually, having realised that despite any advice, here was a lady with mind made up, it was arranged that Nancy would come to the Saturday morning opening of the bank, and the requested large sum would be bagged up and ready for her. She politely declined the offer of having the money delivered to her home but did, however, agree to the suggestion that Michael might accompany her on her walk home; and subsequently, this is what happened. Neither of them realised, at the time, the significance of this decision, or the importance in the fact that Rick also lived in Hartley Road and by chance happened to see Nancy and Michael.

Michael

That Michael was around on a Saturday was in itself unusual, as he still returned home most weekends.

And who knows why he decided to go down into town in the evening? Perhaps it was due to an increase in confidence after being given responsibility earlier in the day.

He knew where he wanted to eat and everything was fine until suddenly he was aware of unwelcome company on either side … two of his King William "mates".

Unwanted by Michael, they apparently wanted him to join them at a party. Feeling pressurised and with a lot less confidence, Michael felt it was safer to go along with them.

Michael had not eaten all day and was definitely not in the habit of excessive indulgence with alcohol. With "help", his tongue gradually loosened and, encouraged by his three so-called friends, the third now having joined them, in no time he was into discussing bank affairs. Unfortunately for Michael, one of the "friends", who actually lived in the same road as Miss Ingram, had seen him earlier in the day, and it was not long before Michael shared details of his mission of importance.

Then all too soon the "good" feeling was overtaken by the complete opposite.

In a state of collapse, Michael was assisted out of the pub and just dumped, left slumped against the wall while the other three young men moved on.

The only bit of good fortune for Michael came in the fact that, much later, one of the voluntary street pastors recognised him and arranged for his transport back to the hostel.

Nancy, Jason, Michael and David have now come together, linked, not only by their city of residence, but about to be linked further through the happenings of one Sunday in October.

OCTOBER 2005

Nancy Ingram folded the foil round the pile of banknotes. The decision had been made and she intended to stick with it. She carefully placed the mini silver brick in the white carrier bag.

The excitement was clear in the two bright eyes that smiled back at her from the hall mirror.

She tucked the soft purple scarf neatly inside the collar of her closely fitting coat and pulled her hat well down over her ears.

'And there's no one now to tell me what I can or can't do!'

She addressed her reflection with an air of defiance. Any other day, she might have added that the loneliness was something else, but this afternoon, Nancy's thoughts were very positive.

Bus pass safely pocketed, gloves on and, struggling to control her umbrella, Nancy, plus bag of goodies, was off to catch the 2.40pm into town.

Where would Harry be today? She had come to quite enjoy the challenge of locating him… it might be tricky today as he would have chosen somewhere out of the rain if he had any sense.

Nancy didn't know the real name of this young man who, five months ago, had suddenly become a part of her life. A chance happening? Some people would say it was meant to be, but Nancy remained open-minded. All she knew was that she did not shop on Sundays out of principle, but on that occasion, she had chosen to take a short cut across the precinct on her way to the central church's tea. Somehow her attention had been drawn to the young man seated with his back to the wall, begging receptacle at the ready. Despite being clearly very "down and out", he reminded her of Harry… that other Harry, who might have… but all that was a long time ago.

From that first encounter, the "now" Harry had continued to bother Nancy, not physically but emotionally. He had probably been like any one of the small children she had known, full of hope and expectation. What had happened?

Over the weeks, her vivid imagination had created a variety of scenarios, provoking a mixture of anger and tears. Nancy's simple response was, however, the provision of a regular Sunday bag of food. Not that she received any sign of gratitude, but that didn't matter.

'But it's not enough,' her conscience nagged at her, 'sandwiches, fruit and homemade cake won't get him out of this mess!'

He needed money. She had money.

She'd made a bold decision.

That morning, Jason got very wet before he sat down. He chose his spot carefully. The roof overhang provided some protection and he was out of the wind.

He never made any effort to tidy himself these days. He slept in his clothes, and he did not smell nice.

Sunday sympathy shoppers were the best… even better if he'd had a dog. Funny how people responded to dogs!

The day passed slowly. With a degree of regularity, coins dropped into the battered cap, just as he had expected… there was certainly one plus about rotten weather… people felt sorrier for you.

By mid-afternoon, he was sure he'd done pretty well. He was contemplating leaving when the white carrier bag came into view.

Nancy had guessed right. The rain had nearly stopped and she actually found him easily.

Jason was surprised to see the old bat out on such a miserable afternoon… you'd got to hand it to her, she was persistent.

He watched as she crossed the precinct towards him. Chin resting on bent knees, he always found it best to avoid eye contact. The feet stopped just in front of him. Goodness, they were small. He hadn't realised quite how skinny her legs were. Bet those shoes cost a bit. Bloody "do-gooders" made him so mad! What did she know? Warm, comfortable home and family. Even his great-aunt Vera had gone and died when he needed her most. It wasn't fair!

In the past, he'd resisted the urge to tell her just what he thought of her ruddy triangle sandwiches and fruit cake. He lived in the night shelter, not the bloody Ritz! Even getting angry was an effort now. The past months seemed to have sapped his spirit.

The bag was beside him and she was off. Had he murmured a "thank you"? He wasn't sure… probably not. He watched as she made her way across to the corner and disappeared. He'd never really noticed how she moved before... strange how someone her age could appear so confident. Would he ever find confidence again?

Why not?

Perhaps he might try a shower this evening, and maybe he could find some new underwear in the store cupboard. And tomorrow... how come he was thinking about tomorrow?

He knew the answer in one word: *Joanne!*

Unlikely she would be on duty Monday, but hopefully he'd see her on Tuesday as usual and tell her about his decision to join the woodwork group. But just as quickly, negative thoughts threatened to replace the positive dreams as reality returned.

He shivered. It was definitely time to move.

It was also time for the 139 to make its way back up the hill.

Nancy Ingram, seated with hands clasped loosely in her lap, gazed out of the window into the darkness, and wondered.

Jason stood up. He was stiff. He stretched his aching back, flexed his knees, walked to the nearby litter bin and tipped in the contents of the white carrier bag. The strong bag would act as his portable safe as usual.

Who was to know that on Monday morning at 7.27am precisely, due to natural curiosity, David Spriggs, refuse collector, would discover something that could make a considerable difference in his life!

★

At about the same time as Nancy and Jason were making their moves, Michael was at last finding himself fully back in the land of the living, having experienced what he could only describe as hell on earth! He was struggling to piece together details of what had happened the previous evening and realising that he must sort himself out before work in the morning.

★

And, not very far away, three other young men were actively involved in making plans for the evening ahead.

PART TWO

Three hooded figures.

One poorly secured back door.

Dead easy!

Door opened and inside.

Now where would she have put the money?

She had it in a bag… a sort of bank bag.

Open drawers… open cupboards… what about that container on the side? No!

'My nan puts…' Not in the fridge.

Into the hallway. Coat and hat hanging on a sort of stand… table… drawer empty… no sign of the money.

Rick, who had seen Michael with Nancy, went straight upstairs… after all, he lived in this road and knew the layout of the bedrooms … which room did she sleep in? He carefully started to investigate.

Downstairs, they moved to the first room… plenty of potential… open everything; drawers, sideboard… where was that bag?

Did she perhaps have a safe? …seemed unlikely.

As they moved towards the front room, the two young men were completely unaware that the second previously undiscovered element of the house was about to materialise.

They had presumed that an old woman would be in bed at this time, and that would normally have been the case but, for Nancy, this had been anything but a normal day.

She had returned home, as usual, hung up her coat and hat and with a feeling of great satisfaction in a job well done, made herself a cup of tea and taken it into the lounge ready to watch *Songs of Praise*. She had, however, done just one extra thing before settling into her favourite armchair. She had taken down a very special photograph from its customary place and lovingly carried it to share this moment with her.

But all too quickly, the euphoria of the moment must have been overtaken by the need for sleep.

So completely unaware of any of this, with sole purpose to find the money, the lounge door was pushed open and first one, then the other stepped into the room and immediately found themselves looking at… well, what appeared to be a lifeless body slumped in a chair. The small amount of light from an outside street lamp filtering in through the narrow gap in the curtains, together with a table lamp on the sideboard, cast an added eerie feel to the room.

'Bloody hell.'

'What the? The old bird's in here!'

'Rick! Come down. Quick!'

The shouts together with the noise of descending feet had an immediate effect.

The "body" moved.

Well, rather, Nancy stirred and with eyes struggling to open, attempted to focus on what was going on.

Then one thing followed another… a scream and cry of horror… a movement in then out of the chair… a crash as a framed photograph hit the television screen… and finally the "body" itself, standing, then staggering, finally collapsing to the floor, finding a resting place lying in the contents of what was actually a cup of tea, between the small overturned side table and the armchair.

There followed a series of groans… then silence.

All this happened fairly quickly while the watchers… just watched!

And then, suddenly no longer made of stone… they fled.

★

On certain roads, there is a great deal of neighbourliness, or some might prefer to call it nosiness. In this case, the former bore fruit.

In the early hours of Monday morning, the sight of an ambulance outside number 18 with blue lights flashing prompted an interested response from a number of fellow residents of Hartley Road.

Knowledge shared later revealed that Mr and Mrs Hodges, who lived immediately opposite Nancy, had been concerned that is was unusual in that the curtains were pulled downstairs but not in the bedroom upstairs. It was a little uncertain as to why they had even looked out of the window at all; there was some suggestion of being woken by the phone ringing, but most felt that was a dream. Suffice to say that Nancy was such a creature of habit that they were concerned enough to investigate further, and of course they quickly discovered the back door open and Nancy on the lounge floor.

Joanne, nearing the end of her A & E night duty, was one of the team receiving an elderly lady around 6 am on Monday morning.

Further up the hill, Hartley Road became a crime scene. A police presence was set up and questioning began. The ever-ready reporters, hopeful for a good story, were rewarded with brief information that appeared as follows in the "Stop Press" of the local evening paper:

> *During the early hours of this morning, police were called to investigate an apparent break-in in a quiet cul-de-sac in the south of the city. They discovered the elderly resident, a female, lying on the floor. There was clear evidence that this was a robbery that may have gone wrong. The police are interested to hear from anyone who can provide any information. More detail will be revealed later.*

*

It was clear that the proverbial grapevine had already been in action once the bank opened to welcome a few early customers.

Behind the counter, Michael tried hard to concentrate on the day's work. He was still feeling the after-effects of Saturday night. Bank manager Frank identified that the usual enthusiasm for the job was sadly lacking. If he hadn't known the lifestyle of the family so well, he might have suspected the results of a hangover, but this seemed out of the question with Michael. He was obviously just a bit under the weather… perhaps he really should allow for this young man to experience an occasional mood swing. He'd just keep an eye on things.

The information that he was picking up through neighbourhood information overheard and clearly shared within his hearing, pushed the problem of Michael way back, as he realised the serious news concerning one of his treasured customers. Did they know about the money? It could have some bearing. He should inform the local police. He made the call.

Shortly afterwards, a casually dressed visitor, actually a plain-clothes officer, being ushered into the bank's inner sanctums, would have attracted very little attention on a Monday afternoon. He had come in response to the call made to the station earlier in the day suggesting possible relevant information regarding the incident in Hartley Road.

To hear that Nancy had withdrawn quite a considerable sum of money certainly demanded further attention.

The obvious question as to how many people in the bank knew about this received a clear answer: 'Nobody except Michael who had acted as a safeguarding escort home, but there could be no question regarding his honesty,' adding quickly, 'and even he didn't know details of the withdrawal value.'

Thanking Frank for his help, the visitor left the bank as discreetly as he had arrived, leaving Frank to focus his thoughts on what had actually happened to Nancy.

★

Deep in thought could also be a description to be attached to David Spriggs, returning home at Monday teatime.

David was never very talkative when he came in from work, and Michelle had learned over the years to give him space. He would usually respond to anything the children wanted to share, but most days the family would exist independently until food was up. Michelle wondered if perhaps he wasn't feeling well, because on this occasion, on arrival, he went straight up into the bedroom and remained there for quite some time. She knew from experience just to wait for any explanation.

The meal passed with very little conversation, younger members only too eager to get back to their own rooms and computer games, with just a cursory nod to homework reminders, leaving Michelle wondering if David was simply tired after a long day. He had gone in early to do a bit extra before going out for collections. So it was that she let it rest.

The night passed and Tuesday began in the usual way but unknown to her at that moment was due to end in a very different way.

★

As David went off to work in the centre of town, higher up the hill, the small early morning-prayer group that Nancy often attended gathered as usual. The news had clearly reached the vicar, and he readily shared concern with the members of the group, concluding with the words:

'And we remember our dear friend Nancy Ingram, praying for a speedy recovery.'

Conversation followed.

'I don't know what the world's coming to when you're not safe in your own home.'

'This was always such a nice area.'

'My mother would turn in her grave hearing about what's happened to Nancy.'

'Your mother… What d'you think Nancy's mother would think? Such a gentle lady.'

'I'd lock 'em all up and throw away the key! Fancy doing that to a frail old lady!'

'Don't think Nancy'd like to hear herself described like that.'

'Well, it's the truth. We're all getting on a bit.'

'I'm surprised she didn't die with the shock!'

'How old is Nancy?'

'Seventy something, I think.'

'She always gives the appearance of being younger. No sign of rheumatics taking over. Not like me. My knees can't cope with the prayers now.'

They reached the church door where the vicar was offering his usual farewell.

'Thank you, vicar. Awful news about Nancy.'

'Certainly. Certainly. But we can't be quite sure what happened until we get further details. One thing we can be sure of is that she's in good hands now. We must keep her in our prayers.'

And with that, he was moving to attend to securing the premises while the stalwart prayerful ladies continued to explore the topic of the moment.

'There's Maisie talking with Nancy's neighbour. Let's see if we can find out a bit more… when Nancy was actually found.'

'And what's this I heard, something about money?'

'A woman in the Co-op said she saw Nancy going to catch the bus into town on Sunday afternoon. I know it's none of my business but…'

★

What could be described as an unexpected onslaught of words bombarded David's ears on Tuesday.

'Poor old soul!'

'Look at this, David!'

She thrust the paper in the direction of her husband who had just walked in through the door.

'David!'

What was up with him?

'Have you seen the paper? Look at this picture on the front page. It's awful. No respect for anyone these days. Bet it was some gang or other. It says they found her lying in a pool of blood.' She paused for just enough time to take a breath.

'David! You're not listening. I'm talking to you…'

Truth was he was far too preoccupied to concentrate on the rantings of his wife.

Instead: 'Where are the kids?'

'Surely you remember they were going to Mum and Dad's for tea and stay the night,' and then, with a little more concern in her voice, bearing in mind her thoughts from the previous evening, 'is anything wrong?'

'No, I'm fine. It's just been a rather hectic day. I think I'll go up and run a bath before we eat.'

And with that, he was on his way upstairs, leaving a rather uncertain Michelle still clutching the evening paper and waiting for the early evening local news programme.

★

Joanne arrived for her Tuesday afternoon shift as day centre nurse.

How many smelly feet, sceptic areas or skin conditions would she meet today? Matted hair… ill-fitting clothes… several days' stubble… lingering aroma of alcohol… they were all second nature now… so very different from the constant pressure of health and hygiene targets held before everyone at the hospital.

The age of some of her patients here defied belief. How could people so young have fallen into such a state of… yes, depredation was the word… and how could apparently old men still be actually under forty? It was all so sad.

But then there was Jason.

She had first met Jason when she was called upon to remove a very large splinter that had become infected. While clearing up the surrounding mass of puss, firmly holding his hand and keeping check for signs of patient in danger of flaking out – something which happened quite frequently amongst people living rough – she had felt an unexplainable attraction.

The question "Why?" had bothered her at first… as if she might be the one to discover the answer to an age-long question.

Until... undoubtedly, "the eyes have it". This was her conclusion. She smiled as she recalled how it sounded like the resolution of a parliamentary debate. For her it had happened in a flash... in no way a well-thought-out resolution ... just the nearness of two people's eyes meeting in what could only be described as a rather unusual setting. Nurse and patient, a well-trodden path to romance in a hospital setting, but she and this Jason... No!

Yet the area of friendship had developed. In no way had there been any compromise in her attention to others. A nurse was there to care and share her medical skills where possible and Joanne gave equally to everyone. But she had started staying on after completing the necessary paperwork. A cup of tea at first meant a chance to just check up on Jason. Then, she had to admit, she began to really look forward to their time together. He had relaxed a bit as well. He had not reached rock bottom... yet... perhaps she could help him to find his way out of this place. There were opportunities but...

Forcibly attacking her apron strings on this Tuesday afternoon, she was only too aware of the inner challenge, *Com' on, Joanne. Be honest. You really fancy this guy!*

A short time later, she was somewhat surprised when the third patient through the clinic door was Jason, clutching a copy of the evening paper. She turned in concern seeing his agitated state.

'I need to talk to you, Joanne,' and as she made eye contact, 'not now, not here. Can we find somewhere quiet when you finish please?'

A local happening has the power to engender a lot of interest. Information can be gleaned in a variety of ways, but anyone without personal knowledge must rely on the media; in this case, the evening paper or the local TV news bulletin.

Although termed an evening paper, an early edition was available at lunchtime. Tuesday's front page had the dramatic headline "Pensioner Left For Dead" followed by the story of the break-in, accentuating distaste at what had happened, described as a horrendous attack on a local resident, by displaying a photograph of the scene and another of senior citizen Nancy Ingram, a picture taken on a much happier occasion. The article contained the suggestion that Nancy may have withdrawn a considerable sum of money from the bank recently, referred to her church involvement with homeless people and also the fact that the police were in possession of an interesting photograph. Again, there was the repeated request for any information that might help the police with their enquiries.

More people tuned in to the early evening local news and listened as the police officer assigned to the case gave an account of being called by a neighbour who had discovered the break-in. In a normal, concise manner, he described the signs of intended robbery and the discovery of an elderly woman lying on the lounge floor. It was uncertain at this moment in time whether anything had actually been taken, although they were following up several possible leads. He was unable to disclose a name or the present condition of the victim. He did confirm that it appeared the intruders left in a hurry. He added that the police were proceeding with enquiries and again requested that anyone with information should make contact. The reporter then interviewed Nancy's next door neighbour, who stressed horror that such a thing should happen to such a lovely lady in their quiet road.

Anyone ready to aid the police with their enquiries?

There were certainly a number of people in possession of information, wondering whether to engage a listening ear. It may raise a smile if the most appropriate comment might be, "To speak or not to speak?" That was the question: a genuine dilemma being faced at this moment in several areas. People whose lives now linked together, finding themselves challenged to face the future.

At the beginning of this story, you were invited to get to know four people but, as happens in life, it is impossible to live life in isolation. It is clearly now the case that considerably more than four people are involved in making decisions on actions to be taken regarding the way ahead, while ironically the person around whom the narrative is built is at this moment lying in a hospital bed, the one person completely unable to have any physical influence.

★

Dan, Rob and Rick had kept clear of each other; a sensible decision just in case anyone had noticed their somewhat unguarded flight. Of course, they were able to keep in touch by phone, limited at first but later the lines became hot.

Questions travelled backwards and forwards. Obvious answers were not forthcoming.

Had anybody seen them?

Living in the same road, Rick faced the greatest challenge. He had managed to slink back indoors without any problem much later in the evening, as his family seldom noted his arrival home.

'Did we drop anything in the rush that could link us to the break-in?' Dan, who always took the lead in the group, continued to assert authority here, clearly referring to his ever-present lack of belief in police expertise.

'What about the old woman?'

This was the major consideration in the minds of Rick and Rob.

'How badly injured is she?'

'Should we tell someone?'

Dan managed to stress the need to avoid detection so forcibly that they finally agreed to carry on with life as usual on Monday morning.

Unknown to the others, after struggling with his conscience, in the early hours of the morning, Rick had actually dialled up the family who lived down the road opposite Nancy in the forlorn hope of alerting them to the situation, but he had hung up without making contact.

★

Jason was waiting for Joanne as she completed her surgery time. The dining area was somewhat limited but he had secured one of the small corner tables. He hardly allowed her time to sit down as he thrust a copy of the paper in front of her, not realising that Joanne had already seen it.

'She didn't look like that when she was brought in.'

Totally shocked, Jason, who had spent the afternoon planning how to share his concern with this now trusted friend, stared at her in silence.

'I was just finishing my A & E session when the ambulance arrived. Poor old soul!'

Still no response from Jason.

'She was moved to intensive care… I'll check on her tomorrow. Now what was it you wanted to talk to me about?'

Jason once more very alive, paper in hand, 'Have you read what it says here? Somebody has suggested that she regularly met a homeless person.'

Joanne waited.

'And it says something about possible missing money.'

'Jason. Stop! I'm not sure what this is all about.'

She made to pick up her mug of tea.

'Joanne! It's her! You know the one I told you about… brought me sandwiches and cake on Sundays.'

Yes, he had mentioned a someone in not-too-flattering tones.

'I saw her on Sunday! Well, I saw her feet and she left the usual white bag.'

And Joanne suddenly became aware of the reason behind his urgency to speak with her as in her mind she linked together the written word and a very distressed Jason.

★

David Spriggs was having trouble sleeping.

They had gone to bed after watching the late news… only a brief reference relating to local ongoing police enquiries. If only Michelle had refrained from mentioning the paper's lead story again as they went upstairs. It was as he had read the whole article in detail on the inside page that the moment of horror had struck him. Hardly surprising that he couldn't sleep. He was aware that the bedside clock had moved into the first hour of Wednesday as he went over and over things in his mind. So many "Whys?" kept surfacing.

'Michelle, I need to talk with you.' He quietly shook his sleeping wife.

Michelle, perhaps not so deeply asleep herself, responded quickly as she was now sure her worst fears were being realised: David was ill!

As she sat up, she realised that David was actually on his hands and knees in front of the fitted wardrobe. He appeared to be attempting to retrieve something from deep inside.

Perhaps he wasn't ill. Perhaps it was…

She waited in the semi-darkness. What was it… some sort of package?

David placed it on the bed and, almost reverently, peeled back the foil to reveal… banknotes! A lot of banknotes. Even in this light, she could see that the one on the top was a £50 note.

What the… clearly a considerable pile, indicating the likelihood of a large sum of money resting on the duvet.

She looked at David for an explanation, and it poured out. Well, one clear statement followed by a whole list of "Whys?"

The extra shift on Monday had meant emptying the bins in the precinct.

Why had his attention been drawn to the foil package?

Why had he brought it home once he had discovered the contents?

Why had he hidden it?

Why hadn't he told Michelle?

Why had he given way to his imagination of what this could mean for the family?

How much money was there now seemed immaterial… it wasn't his!

One featured question word was now replaced by another: 'What can I do, Michelle?'

Michelle could see he was distraught. She was out of bed in a flash, her arms flung round him, and together they clung to each other.

Then very calmly came the words: 'We'll go to the police together in the morning.'

★

The hours of sleep lost by a number of people reached even higher proportions as Michael joined the insomniacs.

All day, he was bombarded by worrying thoughts that persisted once the working day was over; concern about anything he might have said during Saturday's disgraceful happening. That was the only way he could describe it. If only he could remember what he had said.

He had survived Monday at work in a sort of dream existence. Today had been so difficult, overhearing numerous conversations about the happening while all the time facing inner questioning.

Both evenings, he had avoided going to the pub just in case Dan, Rick and the other guy might be there. He couldn't risk facing them.

As so often happens during the hours of darkness, he came to a decision… he would speak with Mr Johnson in the morning.

'You're early, Michael. Couldn't you sleep?'

A slightly weighted question on his behalf as, although he had noted an improvement on Tuesday, Michael was clearly functioning below par.

He was, however, totally unprepared for the one-word answer, 'No,' but then ready for the follow-up. 'I need to talk with you, sir, please.'

Same inner room that represented the beginning of things going so well now threatened to destroy his confidence; he was back in the headmaster's study. As he told the story, he stressed his fear that he may have been responsible for the dreadful things that had happened to lovely Miss Ingram.

Frank listened and remained silent for some time.

All sorts of memories flooded in. He really liked this young man and had been so pleased to witness his confidence develop with guidance from a very shaky start… the customers liked his friendly but polite approach.

A young man stood before him, head hung low, struggling to hold back the tears; could it be reminding him too of a headmaster's office years ago?

The way ahead was his responsibility now.

'I think it would be best if we went and spoke to the police together after the bank has closed.'

The words were out… the day had begun.

★

Both the Wednesday paper and the local TV news again referred to the police following up certain leads. They were now able to confirm a hospital statement that Nancy Ingram's condition remained stable. The one addition to the text on this occasion was to request any information regarding a small black and white photograph of two people and a horse that was found at the scene and clearly printed alongside the article.

★

The interview room at the police station proved very popular on Wednesday, beginning with a very early visit from David and Michelle. After registering their reason for coming with the officer on reception duty, in each case, the visitors sat and waited, usually in silence, to be called.

The procedure then followed the same format:

Two officers, one to question, one to write notes as required, plus agreement that the interview could be recorded, none of which encouraged a feeling of ease, despite the reassuring words of the officer.

Once details of names and address had been recorded, David told the story of finding the package, that now sat on the desk, in a bin very early on Monday morning and foolishly secreting it, hoping to use the contents to the benefit of his family.

Michelle, seeing her husband's obvious distress, jumped in quickly, assuring the officer that this was totally out of character as her husband had an exemplary trustworthy record of employment.

There followed a series of questions and comments with a concluding statement that the object in question, in light of its value, would be held by the police pending the discovery of ownership.

They would be kept informed of the outcome.

All parties then shook hands. It was a very relieved David Spriggs who left the station arm in arm with his wife, no longer weighed down with guilt.

Arriving slightly later, another couple, Jason and Joanne, awaited their turn in the interview room.

The original interview here would obviously not be so straightforward. Jason was sure that any questioning would be biased by the fact that he gave his address as the night shelter.

At their meeting the day before, Jason, without taking a breath and in his feeling of desperation, had gone on to tell Joanne about being given a white bag each Sunday by the woman in the picture, and the bit about money missing, and they were sure to find him and blame him and what if she died and… Joanne, recognising his state of fear, had quietly used her nursing knowledge and gently placed a hand across his mouth. How ironic it was that she had actually been in the hospital at that time.

Once he had calmed down, she had wanted to hear what really happened on Sunday.

Only then, amongst everything else, did Jason tell her that since he had met her, his attitude to life had changed somewhat. He had begun to think there was a future for him and in that connection had taken a lot more interest in support being offered and had joined the woodwork group. On Sunday, although still seated waiting for other people to provide money in sympathy, he had been thinking about future possibilities, and that was probably why he had actually thrown away the belittling gift of food in the bin.

And now he was going to be accused of...

Joanne had once again stemmed the flow with the question, 'Do you still have the white carrier bag?'

Joanne had learned that said article, money donations removed, was now holding articles of clothing waiting for Jason's turn with the washing machine.

Eyes meeting eyes, they had made the decision to go to the police together in the morning, taking the duly emptied white carrier bag in support of their story.

Without doubt, the support and presence of Joanne made it possible for Jason to share his story with the police officer and respond honestly to points and questions raised. The formally aggressive "It's not fair" attitude seemed to have been considerably diluted. He even found himself wanting to apologise to the lady now lying in a hospital bed for the way in which he had previously thought of her. The white carrier bag had somehow become so significant.

The officer in charge summed up the interview by thanking them for coming in with this information, which would be noted in case any connection with the incident was discovered. He decided that he would keep the white carrier bag.

Once again, polite handshakes all round, and Joanne and Jason walked out of the station together with plenty of questions about the future. The room space was now left vacant for yet more visitors who would share information later in the day.

Only a few minutes separated the arrival of two further couples with information to share, but fortunately they did not meet in the foyer as Mr Johnson and Michael were ushered straight into the interview room on account of the earlier visit to the bank.

If the bank manager's office could previously be equated with the headmaster's room, where Michael now found himself was definitely "in court". Whatever would his father say about this?

Formalities concluded, and almost in a daze, he heard Mr Johnson explain that there was something Michael needed to share which they felt might have some bearing on the unfortunate happening. In a firm but quiet, nonthreatening voice, the officer seated at the table invited Michael to tell him what he knew, assuring him that he could take his time… there was no rush.

And Michael did just that. He told him about Saturday night, pausing from time to time to seek reassurance from Mr Johnson. He attempted to tell as much as he could remember from the unexpected meeting, being taken to the pub and the considerable number of drinks, some of which he thought he must have paid for. He said that he wasn't used to drinking alcohol as his family disapproved. It was only to his horror that he later realised he had talked freely about his special assignment on Saturday morning escorting Miss Ingram home safely because she had withdrawn a lot of money. When asked further about this, he confirmed that, as he best recalled, his companions seemed particularly interested in this. He concluded, 'So I started to wonder if I had said something that led to what happened, and it was when I couldn't stop thinking about it that I had to tell Mr Johnson about Saturday night.'

Once again, with notes taken and recording terminated, gratitude was expressed, especially to Michael for his courage in coming forward; and with handshakes all round and an assurance to Mr Johnson that he would be informed of any developments, they were free to go.

Two figures seated in the foyer kept a very low profile as, to their horror, they both independently recognised Michael while he, keen to get away from the place, hurried out without glancing left or right.

Rob and Rich had come to the station after considering the trouble they were in. Let's be honest, they were scared. It surely wouldn't be long before somebody identified them. Together with Dan, they were known in the village. That was it. Before Dan, it had been different. Above all else, their main concern was the condition of the old woman with the totally horrendous thought, *What if she should die!* Could they then be accused of murder?

They were kept waiting for some time where every minute seemed like an hour. At last, the moment came when they were invited to come on in and then, something obvious but in their present state of mind completely unexpected, they were taken into two separate interview rooms.

It is probably enough for you to know that both interviews were carried out sympathetically and were really just an opportunity for each young man to tell the story of what happened on Sunday night and gradually with gentle questioning to build up the picture of all that had happened before the break-in, beginning with their first meeting with Michael. Once returned to the foyer to continue their waiting, they remained in silence without attempting to compare notes; just eye contact in an attempt to reassure each other. Elsewhere, notes were compared which, allowing for a few minimal discrepancies, lined up, leaving the interviewing officers in agreement that it was the third member of the group that they needed to speak with since it became clear that it was his arrival on the scene that had brought about a change in the behaviour of these two young men, who were thanked for coming in with their information and advised that they were free to go but that they might be called back if necessary.

Once outside, Rob and Rich now had an extra worry: about how to cope when they next met Dan.

★

A single lady and an only child, Nancy was without immediate family. However, being well known and loved, she received numerous cards and visits in hospital, even possibly too many of the latter in the early stages. Both the vicar and her next door neighbour could be relied upon for updates. Being made of tough stuff, she was not going to allow this one unpleasant incident to ruin her life; however, it was clear that time would be needed to restore both body and mind. One visit that at the time proved both very special and in some ways confusing was when Jason met Joanne outside the hospital and together they visited Nancy. The visit seemed to create what could be described as near joy for Nancy, while for Jason, gentle agreement seemed the best way to respond to her confusing suggestion that the gift of money would help him to move on. Together, they decided that Nancy's thinking was still very mixed up.

A whole group of people were now waiting on the outcome of recent events; in most cases, uncertain about what lay ahead. Completely unknown to any of them, someone else would shortly be joining the list.

*

Alison had spent Wednesday in Bath following up a piece of information which would definitely need a further visit. This prompted the germ of an idea of possibly linking the weekend with Graham in the city. She purchased a local paper to read on her train journey home. Although Salisbury was not far away, she didn't get many opportunities to visit the place that had long-ago family associations. Front page and following pages presented little interest. She turned to page five where it was not a headline but rather a small photograph that instantly grabbed her attention. She had seen it before, or rather, she had seen the same photograph and was actually in possession of its twin. Reading the accompanying story, Alison discovered that the police were seeking any information relating to this photograph since it featured in a local crime investigation, details of which she then read with interest.

Once home, Alison very quickly went to the spare room and from the bottom drawer in the filing cabinet lifted out the small cardboard box that she had found amongst her father's possessions following his death. Downstairs again, from the collection of, obviously once valued, items within, she took out a small black and white photograph. It matched the one in the newspaper.

When Graham came in, about half an hour later, he found his wife sitting with a newspaper sort of on her lap. It was clear that she had been crying. It was as he moved to place a comforting arm around her shoulders that he became aware of what was clutched in her hand. A photograph… that, on close inspection, he had never seen before.

Gradually, the story of finding the box containing a few items that it seemed had special significance for her father.

Why hadn't she shown it to him before?

She didn't have an answer except somehow it had presented a very personal link.

And the photograph?

Yes. She had seen it but until this moment it had remained in the box; just an old photograph somehow associated with her father's past.

Sharing the newspaper item together helped to clear away any remnant of tears, and they moved on to find something to eat before addressing the next move.

Quietly studying the photo, their attention moved to the back, something that had been inexplicably overlooked until this moment.

And they read, *Somerset Stakes… Future Promise with Nancy.*

It didn't take long to come up with a possible horse racing link and, using modern technology, to discover that the Somerset Stakes had been an annual event at Bath Racecourse, still linked to the present day.

At this moment, any clear connection between the two photographs eluded them both, but they agreed that Alison would respond to the police request by calling in at the local station on Friday.

So here, in a slightly different context, was that suggested someone else added to the list of those waiting and wondering.

Alison's business was completed fairly easily on Friday morning, and it was well before midday that she found herself in the interview room at the police station. She was completely devoid of the apprehension of the other interviewees relating to this case. She was under no pressure; just very eager to know more than she had learned from the paper.

Welcome and identities confirmed, Alison produced her father's photograph.

Clearly, the two photographs matched. Then interest turned to the details on the back of each.

Side by side on the desk. The writing was obviously the same but the wording slightly different. The officer seated across the desk gave no indication of any particular interest and continued speaking, but as Alison read the previously unseen simple message, *Never to be forgotten. Love, Harry*, emotion took over. In a moment, what to Alison, bearing in mind her natural sense of inquiry engendered by her occupation as a solicitor, had previously been an interesting story in a newspaper, suddenly took on a whole new significance It became real. And she was part of it. "Nancy", the name common to both newspaper and photo, who previously hadn't fully registered with her, turned into a real person. Clearly, she had been blinkered… she smiled… rather an appropriate thought regarding a horse picture.

The interviewing officer, realising that her thoughts were elsewhere, paused and waited. Alison, with apologies, clicked back into the present and listened as he went on to confirm the present situation regarding the breaking and entering situation, stating that they were now in possession of several helpful pieces of information and concluding that they were holding an item pending ownership. The only major anxiety of the moment surrounded the condition of Miss Ingram who was, thankfully, not in any obvious life-threatening situation, despite all that had happened. She was apparently gaining in strength but according to those around her remained very muddled regarding the happenings of Sunday. This mental condition was thought to be the follow-up of the shock, and hopefully things would return to normal, given time. She would certainly remain in hospital for some time yet.

Business concluded and details noted, it was agreed that Alison could hold on to her photograph on the understanding that it would be produced if required at any later date. The officer confirmed that visiting Nancy was quite in order, adding that any further information she might glean could prove useful. They parted with a handshake and a repeated "Thank you" to Alison for her response.

A text to Graham subsequently agreed that he should come straight to meet her in the hospital foyer cafe at about 4pm. This meant that she was free to have a leisurely lunch while contemplating what might lie ahead.

Alison had to confess that she didn't like hospitals. Hospitals carried memories with them and, as seems to be the case with quite a number of people, the bad is often remembered more than the good. She approached the designated ward with a degree of trepidation. The occupant of the bed was not in the bed but rather seated, propped up in an adjacent chair and at this moment was in the act of enthusiastically farewelling a young male and female. The attention immediately switched to Alison, who was entreated to come and meet Harry. In the rather restricted space, the young woman confirmed that they were actually leaving and in no uncertain terms reminded Nancy that two visitors was the limit and that she would see her again soon.

They moved out and Alison moved in.

Knowing that flowers were prohibited in hospital, she placed a *Get Well Soon* card on the bedside table.

'Have you come from the church?' and before she could answer, 'you probably hadn't met Harry before. I see him every Sunday but now that he's got the money, he won't have to beg anymore.'

And still more, hardly pausing for a breath,

'Would you like a grape? People are so kind. What did you say your name was?'

Quickly before she started again,

'I'm Alison and we haven't met before, Nancy.'

'Well, I'm very pleased to meet you, Alison. Did you say you came from the church?'

'No. I just read about your accident in the newspaper.'

A pause and then,

'Harry said he will come and see me when I am back home. That young nurse said they'll let me go home soon… I wonder if Harry knows where I live.'

The police officer's information seemed to hold water. Should she risk introducing the photograph that she held securely within her pocket?

And then as if… could it be an unexplainable moment of telepathy…

'I went to the races with the other Harry. I wonder what happened to him?'

Alison fought to hold back the tears. Nancy and Harry… her dad. Her dad still remembered. She wanted to say, 'I can tell you,' but this was not the moment.

Instead, she managed a

'Can I come and see you again too?' which in response received a smile and a gracious 'Of course you can, dear.'

Alison leaned forward and hugged this rather frail-looking elderly lady, and again, as if it had been planned, a nurse arrived to help Nancy back into bed.

Alison left the ward as the tears broke through, and made her way down into the cafe in the hospital foyer. Graham might be there but it was earlier than planned. She would have a cup of tea while she waited. The young couple, whom she had encountered at Nancy's bedside, were already seated there and beckoned her to join them.

Joanne sort of took charge of the situation once names had been exchanged, including the way in which, due to Nancy's state of confusion, Jason had been called Harry. There seemed to be an immediate rapport between them. She explained how Nancy had been brought into the ward she was on. Gradually, with agreement from Jason, she shared the story of how the two of them had independently become involved with Nancy and with each other.

Alison's attention was fully held as the story unravelled. Quite some story, as yet without an ending, and she had now became part of it.

Then it was her turn. She told how, quite by chance, she had seen the photograph in the paper and had realised it was identical to the one she had at home. At this point, the said treasured item emerged from the secretion of her pocket and she handed it to them. She said that she just knew it was in her father's box but to her knowledge with no obvious reason for it being there. Responding to the police request, and in her desire to know more, she had spent an hour or so at the police station with the photo before coming to the hospital.

A few minutes later, Graham arrived and, following introductions, learned that unless he chose otherwise, together with Alison they would be meeting again for lunch the next day. True to character, his wife's unexpected statements had long since ceased to surprise him. Both couples certainly had plenty to discuss independently once they had parted company, but this also marked the beginning of something special between them.

The police were now in possession of a whole lot of statements… all of which, unlike most cases, had come together in quite a short time. As usual, the job of sorting them into some sort of order fell to one officer, who now set about the task in hand.

It was not long before the word "confession" came to mind, and that took him back to… no, that was long ago. Just try to work out the chain of events and the way that the, apparently very different, people had become linked. It was definitely proving very difficult to see how the old photograph could possibly have any significance. At this point, he was not to know that it would be this photo in the hands of a caring solicitor that would be responsible for bringing about a very satisfactory conclusion to the case in the not-too-distant future.

★

Nancy walked into the lounge, placed her mug of tea on the table alongside the waiting slice of fruit cake and settled down in her favourite armchair. She had enjoyed the visit from her new "family" but now was her special thinking time before watching *Songs of Praise*. Alison regularly drove over to see her on a Sunday, and on quite a few occasions, Jason and Joanne had managed to drop in as well. It was surprising how what had happened only a few months ago – that at the time had caused such distress and was now, thankfully, becoming just a memory – had actually proved so beneficial. These three were clearly filling a void in her life that she had never fully realised, and there was also the extra bonus of a personal solicitor.

Once they had been able to prove, aided by Alison's knowledge of the law, that the package of money was clearly intended for Jason, it had all been sorted out. With the need for secrecy removed, she had been able to give Jason the deposit for the flat that he now shared with Joanne and also the money needed for his woodwork apprenticeship. The table on which her mug now resided was an early sample of his handiwork. She smiled. Hopefully, they would continue to find happiness together.

Once released from hospital, after agreeing to an extra fortnight in respite, Nancy had fairly quickly returned to her normal weekly routine. The only difference, as she put it, was she felt rather like a celebrity as now she was recognised by considerably more people than before, after what she termed "the happening". All sorts of people exchanged a smile and a greeting in addition to her friends in the bank, the shop and amongst churchgoers, not forgetting, of course, the support from the Hartley Road neighbours. In this latter connection, it had been strange the way that, shortly after her declining to press charges regarding the break-in, a young man, who lived just along the road, had come forward offering help in her garden. Funny how some people could only see bad in young people.

Nancy's original photograph now occupied central spot on the sideboard. Joanne had chosen the new frame after requesting a copy for her and Jason. To its right, there was now a photograph of the Spriggs family. It had come with a thank you letter, following her decision that David's honesty deserved to be well recognised. She did feel that the rather large, what could best be described as a "wedding-type" hat looked a little out of place, but then it was none of her business.

As she sipped her tea, her eyes were drawn back to the photograph. A simple photograph, marking just one day in her long life and yet a photograph that had come to play a part in the lives of a number of people.

Two young people and a horse.

Nancy smiled again.

'What a pity we didn't have a chance to explore any future promise together, Harry. We might have made a great partnership!'

And then she added, 'But I promise that if my numbers come up again, I will always remember you started it all.'

About the Author

Barabara Shrubsole

Barbara has been retired from primary school teaching for some time and enjoys writing as a hobby.

She moved from Portsmouth to Bath with her husband and family in 1975, and has three married children and seven, now adult, grandchildren.

Barbara is a member of Manvers Street Baptist Church and bases her life on practical Christianity.

She has always spent time in voluntary work and describes herself as a "people person."

At present she is involved in various ways within the Open House Centre.

Barbara has previously self published two books of poems. "Literary Allsorts," a collection of short stories, was commercially published in 2016. "Photo Finish" is a response to the question "What happens next?" relating to one of the stories.